SPECS FOREVER

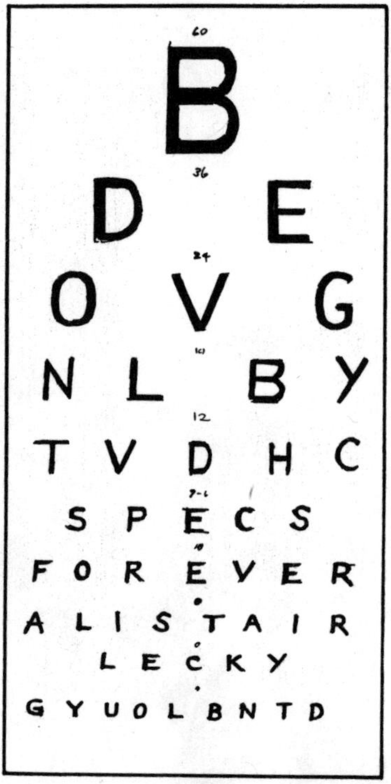
60
B
36
D E
24
O V G
N L B Y
12
T V D H C
S P E C S
F O R E V E R
A L I S T A I R
L E C K Y
G Y U O L B N T D

SPECS FOREVER

by

AGNES SZUDEK

Illustrated by Susan Sansome

HAMISH HAMILTON
LONDON

18106830

First published in Great Britain 1981 by
Hamish Hamilton Children's Books
Garden House, 57–59 Long Acre, London WC2E 9JZ

COPYRIGHT © 1981 Agnes Szudek
Illustrations Copyright © 1981 Hamish Hamilton Ltd

British Library Cataloguing in Publication Data

Szudek, Agnes
  Specs forever. – (Antelope books).
  I. Title   II. Series
  823′.914[J]

  ISBN 0-241-10625-7

Filmset in 'Monophoto' Baskerville by
Eta Services (Typesetters) Ltd., Beccles, Suffolk
Printed in Great Britain by Ebenezer Baylis & Son Ltd.,
The Trinity Press, Worcester and London

Contents

To those with specs who
grin and wear them

Chapter 1
Get Your Specs

ALISTAIR LECKY RACED along the hall and into his bedroom. He stopped in front of the chest-of-drawers and looked at himself in the mirror. He didn't recognise the face that looked

back at him. It couldn't be him. His eyes were circled with brown spectacles and his cropped hair stood up in spikes.

Thumping his fists on top of the chest he shouted between sniffs and tears, "That's not me! That's an owl! A horrible-looking owl with a-a fright!"

He wrenched the spectacles from his ears and flung them on the bed. "I won't wear them! I won't!" In his anger he threw his knitted hat on the carpet, kicked it with his boots, then sent Action Man flying across the room after it.

As he pulled off his anorak and wiped his wet face on the sleeve of his sweater, Aly thought of the years ahead. He would never look the same again, ever. The hair was bad

8

enough, but every day from now on he would have to wear spectacles – things fixed to his face.

Aly's eyes had been bothering him for months. He couldn't see the blackboard clearly but he didn't want to tell anyone. Then, one day Miss Hopper wrote a number test on the blackboard and Aly got nearly all his sums wrong. His teacher called him to her desk.

"Alistair? When did you last have your eyes tested?"

"Er – I don't remember," he said. "When I was in the Infants, I think."

Miss Hopper looked puzzled. "But the optician was here in the summer. What did he say?"

Before Aly could think of an answer a loud voice called out, "He never had his eyes done, Miss." It was Tessie Hogg. She had a memory like an elephant. "He had measles, Miss Hopper. He wasn't here. I can remember."

"Thank you, Tessie. What would I do without you?" Miss Hopper said, patiently.

Then she had written a letter to

Aly's mother about his eyes and his mother had taken him to the optician in the High Street. The man looked into Aly's eyes with a small bright light and afterwards asked him to read the letters on a long chart, like one they had in school. Aly couldn't read the chart very well. The optician said Aly was short-sighted and would have to wear glasses. He called them glasses, but Aly's mother called them spectacles because she said they weren't made of glass any more. Whatever they were called, Aly thought the day he had just collected his specs and had his hair ruined by a strange barber was the worst Saturday ever.

Aly took his Schoolboy's Diary from his pocket and wrote in the space for Saturday, SPECS FOREVER.

As he stuffed the diary back into his pocket he touched something warm and soft. He drew out a squashed Gnu chocolate bar that his mother had bought him on the way home. It was to make up for the specs he thought.

Specs forever

Aly squeezed the Gnu back into its oblong shape, opened the window and put it out on the ledge to cool off. Snow was settling on it as he turned and went out of his bedroom.

On the way to the kitchen, he shut

his eyes and tried to guess what was cooking. Was it peas or beans he could smell? It was a game he had

played with his mother since he was three. Even now in the Junior school he still did it. He and Stevie Short

did it with school dinners. Fish and chips were easy, so were cabbage and cheese pie. At home it was more difficult.

With his eyes closed, he felt for the kitchen door. He shuffled his feet

along in case Ouch, the cat, was in the way, washing as usual. He was almost on to the kitchen tiles when his mother suddenly said, "Alistair! What *are* you doing? Where are your specs?"

Aly stopped with his hands out-stretched. Then his eyes snapped open. He said, "I'm only playing. It's a game, Mum. You know."

But his mother seemed to have forgotten all about their game.

"Get your specs," she said.

"But, Mum. I was only – "

"Get your specs," his mother said again. "It's not nice to play at being blind. Some people are you know. It's not funny. And stop making a song and dance about your eyes."

"It's not a song and dance. It's – " Aly began.

"Get your specs!"

This time his mother sounded really angry. She shook the pot. Aly saw peas in it before she banged it down on the cooker.

Aly turned and went back to his room. This time his eyes were open but still he saw nothing. The walls and floor were sliding up and down, blurred through his tears.

He wished his specs would somehow disappear, like the ones in the play his class had made up for the Christmas concert. It was called *Swig-The-Squinter*. Everything was going wrong for Swig the wizard because he had lost his Hot-Spells-Specs. Miss Hopper had written out the play with ideas from the class. They were going to be given their parts on Monday. Aly loved to act

and hoped he'd get a part. He usually did.

When he went into his bedroom the specs were still there on the bed. He grabbed them roughly and pushed them on. It was true, he could see better with them. They were useful for – for – He was trying to think of the good points about specs when he heard his father come in. "Where's my son?" he was saying. And Aly knew by the sound of his voice there was a big smile on his face. "Come out, come out wherever you are," his father sang out. "I'm coming to get you."

Aly slunk back behind his door. He felt shy. But his father came right in and swung him up in the air.

"Hey – you do look different," he said. "You know, you look like – you look like – "

"You mean an owl. I look like an owl," Aly interrupted.

"An owl? Good heavens, no! You look like a hard-working student. Somebody who knows where he's going in life. And, you look just like that actor on T.V., the boy who played Brains in that series about a gang of children. What was it called?" He couldn't remember and neither could Aly. "Come on, let's eat," his father said. And he carried Aly on his back and dumped him on a chair at the table.

Aly's mother handed round plates

of hamburgers, bacon, peas and potatoes. She said, "You see Alistair, your specs are all right, no need for any fuss."

"I wasn't fussing," Aly muttered under his breath. "But you can't like my hair, Dad. Nobody could like my hair."

"Well, it doesn't look like Sid's work, too short on top." His father ruffled the spiky ends then ate his dinner quickly.

"It wasn't Sid," said Aly's mother. "There were too many people there. I took Alistair to that new place near the bakery, but never again. Just look at it! I think that fellow was more used to clipping dogs. He's like a frightened terrier."

"Owl. More like an owl," Aly mumbled into his dinner.

"Don't worry. Hair grows at two centimetres a month, or thereabouts, I think," Aly's father said, wiping his plate clean with a piece of bread.

Aly's father usually went to a meeting on Saturday nights and to-night he was soon gone, eating a biscuit on the way out. Usually, when Aly and his mother were alone they played games for two like, Othello, Draughts or Fox and Geese, but now when his mother said, "Well, what's it going to be to-night?" Aly didn't want to play anything.

"Nothing thanks," he said.

"Nothing?"

"I don't feel too good. I think I'll go to bed soon."

"Oh, well, suit yourself," his mother said, shrugging her shoulders.

"I'll get on with my sewing. If you feel worse, let me know."

"I'll let you know." Aly pushed his chair back and got up. He lifted Ouch, and carried her in his arms to the sofa. She settled comfortably on his knee and began to purr. "You're lucky," Aly whispered into her soft

pointed ear. "You'll never have to wear specs, unless some clever-Dick invents them for short-sighted cats."

After a while Aly couldn't keep awake and crawled off to bed. It was the earliest Saturday bedtime he could remember.

Chapter 2
I Feel Sick

ALY WOKE EARLY on Monday morning with a sick feeling rolling round in his stomach. For a few seconds his mind was blank. Why did he feel sick? Then the answer struck him like a blow. Today he had to go to school for the first time, wearing specs.

He tumbled out of bed and staggered to the door wondering whether to go to the bathroom and be sick or to try not to be sick. In his half-asleep mind he was aware that he was giving himself a choice. The sickness no longer seemed very real. He crossed the hall to his parents' bedroom. They were both asleep. The alarm clock said ten past six.

Aly tip-toed back to his room, climbed into bed and tucked his knees up to his chest. He lay looking at the yellow wall, imagining all the fingers that would be pointed at him and the hoots of laughter in the playground. He remembered what had happened to Nudge Larkin the day he turned up with a gold brace on his teeth. It glittered when he smiled. The Million Dollar Kid, that's what he was nicknamed, with his mouthful of gold. "Here, like some nougat?" Sorry it's not gold." The boys had taunted Nudge like this every playtime until Aly had stepped in and said, "Nougat and nugget are not even spelt the same. They're different words, so shut up all of you."

For his trouble he got a punch in the back from Reggie Barker that made him swallow his mint. It stuck somewhere in his throat, far down, but it was worth it. Come to think of it, Nudge didn't smile any more. Aly couldn't remember even one big grin from him since that day, and that was three months ago. All the laughter had gone out of him. He was keeping his brace hidden behind a straight face. Aly thought that was one good point about a brace, but specs couldn't be hidden.

At last it was eight o'clock. His mother coughed as she came out of her room. Aly slid down under the covers.

"Time for school, Alistair. Come

on – where are you?" His mother prodded the heap under the quilt until she found Aly's head and un-covered it. "Show a leg, my lad."

"I can't," Aly mumbled.

"Why not? You've still got two, haven't you?" His mother felt for his legs and drew them out sideways. "There they are."

"I feel sick," Aly said, holding his stomach. "I'm sick as anything."

"No wonder, with your head covered up."

Aly moaned and rolled back into bed. "Ooo-oh! I'm too ill to go to school, honestly."

His mother went out of the room and came back with a thermometer. She said, "We'll see if you've got a temperature. Open your mouth." She put the thermometer under Aly's

tongue. "Keep still. I'll be back in a moment."

Aly hoped she was going to ring the school to say he was ill. He listened for the little tinkle of the telephone, but he heard nothing. He tried to make his mouth water, swirling the saliva between his teeth. He hoped he could warm it up and maybe raise his temperature. Keeping his lips pressed tightly together so that no cold air could get in, he tried to think himself into a raging fever.

Within a few minutes his mother came back briskly, like a nurse, as though she'd been taking temperatures most of her life. She neatly drew the thermometer from Aly's mouth, turned it a little and said, "Normal. Just as I thought. Get dressed Alistair. You'll feel better when you've had your breakfast. I'll make boiled egg and toast."

Aly thought the sound of boiled egg and toast made him really want to be sick, right that minute. "Mum, I'm sick. I can't," he said.

"All right, no egg or toast. What about Shreddies, Weetabix or muesli?"

"Ugh – nothing. I'll only bring it up all over the kitchen, I know I will. And Mum, my temperature might shoot right up in school and I'd never get home. Have you thought of that?" Aly clutched the sheet to his chin. "I think I should stay in bed."

"Nonsense," his mother replied. "Miss Hopper will know if you're that ill and I'll come and collect you. Now get dressed Alistair or you'll be late. And – don't forget your specs," she added, pointing to them on the chest of drawers.

By the look on his mother's face, Aly knew there was no use arguing.

He pulled his clothes off the chair and got dressed in bed. Then he lifted the spectacles and tried them against the partly-dressed Action Man. "See, they don't issue kits with specs for you, do they? Only me."

He took the specs to the bathroom where there was a large mirror by the window. He wanted to see exactly what he would look like to his friends – and Reggie Barker who never missed a chance to laugh at anybody. Show-off Reggie with skin like a hippo that nobody could ever crack. Aly knew he would have a field day at the sight of him. He looked worse than he had thought.

His hair *was* too short on top, as his father had said, and it was still sticking up in spikes after two days. His specs curved just where his eyebrows

were so that his eyebrows disappeared. *And* with two front teeth
missing, Aly thought he must be the
ugliest boy in the world. He could
join a circus straight away and let
people pay to come and laugh at
him. Alistair Lecky, a freak you'll
never forget. He put his hands to his
ears and was wiggling his fingers

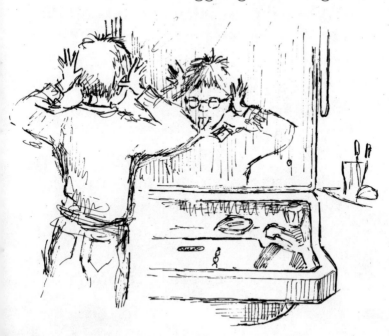

with his tongue out when his mother opened the bathroom door.

She was holding his anorak and school bag. "I'm ready. Let's go or you'll be late. I'll walk you to the school gate today."

Usually his mother saw him across the road as far as the traffic lights, but today she went all the way.

When they reached the school, the classes were already going in. Aly was glad he didn't have to stand in the playground. He went into the cloakroom to hang up his anorak. Stevie was there.

"Hey, Aly!" Stevie took a step back, pretending to be surprised. "When did you get those?"

"Saturday," Aly said, looking at the floor.

"Wow! Poor you! It must be

32

rotten wearing specs. You remind me
of somebody on T.V. Let me think."
Stevie tried to sound kind but it
made Aly feel worse.

"Don't bother! I don't want to
know." Aly's voice was hoarse
and trembling as he pushed past
Stevie.

Aly went towards the classroom.
He paused in the doorway. For once,
Miss Hopper wasn't there.
Everybody was milling about, chat-
ting, sharpening pencils and collect-
ing books. Then they saw Aly. Every
eye seemed to be fixed on him and
fingers pointed.

"Crumbs! Who's that?"

"We've got a new boy, kids."

"Oh, no! We can't squeeze
another desk in here."

"It's only Aly Lecky."

"Specky-Lecky! Hey, Specky-Lecky."

The last voice was Reggie Barker's. Aly knew without even

looking up. He had known it would be like this. His mother could have helped if she had cared about him being sick. He wished he was back home under his bedcovers. Somehow he made his legs carry him miles and

miles to his desk. He dropped onto his chair and put his hands over his ears.

He knew the moment Miss Hopper came in because there was a sudden silence. Everyone obeyed Miss Hopper. She was the kind of teacher

you liked, and wanted to behave for. Aly opened his eyes. She was taking the register out of her desk.

"Sorry to keep you waiting," she said, softly. "Someone wanted to speak to me."

Chapter 3
British Bulldog

ALY FOLDED HIS arms and looked
straight at his teacher, trying to
ignore Reggie Barker who sat in
front of him and was making circles

with his fingers and thumbs – specs for Aly's benefit.

When Miss Hopper came to his name on the register, she looked up at Aly. "Alistair Lecky?"

"Yes, Miss Hopper."

"Glad to see you've got spectacles," she said, smiling. "And children, we've all seen spectacles before, haven't we?" she added, addressing the class. "There's nothing hilariously funny about spectacles, remember." No one dared to laugh.

When she had finished the register, Miss Hopper stood up with a sheet of paper in her hand. "Listen carefully," she said. "I'm going to give out parts for the Christmas concert and we'll have a practice this afternoon. But don't forget, it's only a try-out."

Aly was desperate to be in the play. He wanted the part of Swig the magician, but who didn't! He clenched his fingers together under his desk and bit his lip, willing Miss Hopper to call out his name. He had read something about will-power and how strong it can be, if you try hard enough and have faith. It hadn't worked with his temperature, but it might work this time. "Swig the magician – Alistair Lecky," that's what Miss Hopper was going to say. That would stop Reggie Barker's smirking.

Miss Hopper cleared her throat and began, "Mrs Gumpy – Harriet Wilson, Granny Gossip – Tessie Hogg." Aly knew she was bound to get that part. "The policeman," went on Miss Hopper, "Frank

Joblot, the magician's assistant – Steven Short. And Swig-The-Squinter –." Here she stopped and looked right at Aly.

He began to feel himself turning pink with pleasure. The part was his. She was going to call out his name. She hesitated, then said, "Er – er, well now." Her eyes flickered for a moment, then moved away from Aly. "Mm – ye-es. Swig-The-Squinter, Reggie Barker. The Christmas-Cracker-Creeper – Nessie McIntosh, Sam Bird, Amy Hills, Martin Eke, Flora Wolfe, John Cottle, Norris Larkin and the O'Brien twins. That will do to start with. Now I want you to – "

Aly didn't hear anything else. His fingers became limp under the desk and his jaw dropped. She had been going to chose him. He was sure of it. She almost said, "Alistair Lecky," then she didn't. Aly thought he knew why.

It was his specs. She couldn't bear the sight of him in specs. She just hadn't been able to keep looking at his face with specs, spiked hair, no eyebrows and two teeth missing. Reggie Barker, large and lumpy, was like a dream-boy compared with him.

The rest of the morning was miserable for Aly. At playtime he stood round the corner of the wall behind the toilets. Stevie had a job with the milk crates and Aly didn't want to risk being with anybody else.

But it wasn't long before Reggie Barker and his crowd came racing round the corner, playing *British Bulldog*. When they saw Aly they stopped and crowded round him.

"Look who's here. It's Specky-Lecky, hiding himself away. No wonder!" Reggie jeered.

As Aly flattened himself against the wall, Reggie began to sing,

"What's the matter with Alistair,
He went for a walk and met a bear,
And Alistair gave the bear a scare.
Yeah! Yeah! Yeah!"

43

All the "Yeah, Yeahs" brought
Miss Hopper round the corner. She
chased the children back into the
playground. Then she noticed Aly.

"Run about Alistair, or you'll
catch cold." She spoke gently, even

patted his shoulder, but Aly twisted
his shoulder away.

"I'm not cold," he said, briefly.
She didn't need to think she had to
be kind if she couldn't bear the sight
of him.

45

"Are you all right?" she asked.

"I'm fine," Aly replied. He dived away quickly. He knew she was going to say something else, but he didn't want to listen. She had been his favourite teacher until today. Now he wished he wasn't in her class any more.

Chapter 4
Leave Us The Plate, Mate

AT LUNCH TIME, Aly ate his dinner as slowly as he could, so that he wouldn't have to go out to the playground. The dinner ladies told him to

hurry up and so did Miss Hopper. She was on dinner duty. He didn't seem to be able to get away from her at all. "It's a very good piece of meat," she said. "I don't want you to leave any of that dinner. Remember there are starving children in the world who would be grateful for it." That would have been Reggie Barker's cue to say pertly, "Here y'are then Miss, they can have it."

"I'll eat it all." Aly said. And he scraped every little bit of cold gravy on to his fork, trying to suck it off before it dropped. He did the same with his custard. Every speck of yellow was spooned up until Mrs Pearce, the huge dinner lady joked,

"Hang on then! Leave us the plate, mate!"

When Miss Hopper and the child-

ren had gone, Aly rose and carried
his plate to the washing up stack.
Mrs Pearce bellowed in his ear.

"Like to help me put the chairs
away?"

Aly nodded, and by the time he
had done that as slowly as he could,

arranging the chairs in a row round the hall, it was almost one-thirty. Mrs Pearce put her hand in her overall pocket and brought out a Kit Kat. "You're a good boy. That's for missing all your lunch play. Shame eh?" she said, and she winked. Aly thought she knew more than she was saying.

At two o'clock Miss Hopper gave out copies of the play *Swig-The-Squinter* and the class walked to the hall for a practice. First, she pushed the grey medical screen into a corner so that she could see the stage clearly. After that, she told the actors to stand on the stage and everyone else had to sit on the floor cross-legged.

It was the way Reggie Barker swaggered up the steps to the stage that really made Aly angry. He wriggled his bottom about, then turned and put his fingers round his eyes at Aly. He was always a show-off. He had more pocket-money than anybody else, a real leather football, and even a movie camera, so he said. Aly couldn't understand why Miss Hopper had chosen *him* for the best

part. There were other boys in the class.

Aly clenched his fists as if he was ready to give Reggie a punch on the nose. He did it in the air in front of his own face, sparring like a boxer getting ready for a fight, punching and dodging, until someone grabbed his arm.

It was Miss Hopper. "Try to sit still, Alistair. We're going to begin."

Miss Hopper turned her attention to the actors, giving them their places. Aly tried to sit still, but he couldn't. He couldn't look at show-off Reggie, just as his teacher couldn't look at him. He wanted to hide his ugliness somewhere.

Aly looked about for a hiding-place. There was only the long wide hall with the P.E. boxes at the far end and the swing doors. Near the stage was a piano and the grey screen in the corner. Aly looked again at the screen. It was folded, but not quite closed. There might just be enough space to squeeze between the folds.

When no one was looking, Aly slid little by little towards the screen. Miss Hopper's voice sounded impatient in the background. That wasn't like her at all.

"No, Reginald! No, no, no! You take a swig of this and a swig of that and you must show how nasty it is. Now try to look shocked and squint, please, squint! Remember you've lost your Hot-Spells-Specs and you can't see what you're doing. Do it again, please."

Reggie did it again and again and

again, but Miss Hopper was not pleased. Reggie had a cheeky face for a start and he couldn't look shocked or squint. He didn't look at all like a wizard.

"Try, Reginald, just *try*," Miss Hopper pleaded.

"I *am* trying," Reggie said, impudently. "This is just daft, that's all."

For a moment there was a silence so deadly, half a pin would have been heard dropping. Then Miss Hopper said, "Thank you very much, Reginald. That will do." Her voice had gone back to its quiet tone, but there was a sharp coldness about it, as icy as the weather outside. She pointed to a place on the floor. "Sit down. We will try someone else."

"Oh, but that's not fair! Give us a

chance!'' Reggie called out. But Miss Hopper's finger was still pointing downwards. She kept it pointing until Reggie flung himself down on the polished floor, sending two girls sprawling.

While the class nudged each other and murmured about Reggie's rudeness, Aly had moved silently as far as

the screen. One more little slide along the floor and he would be out of sight. Aly slid. He reached the grey metal legs of the screen. With one swift movement he was on his feet.

There was just enough space for him to stand between the folds of cloth. Aly had disappeared.

Chapter 5
Alistair, Where Are You?

ALY HARDLY DARED to breathe inside the screen in case the grey cloth fluttered. Holding his hands over his

nose and mouth, he took short, shallow breaths. His head was beginning to spin with the stuffiness when all at once he gulped with fright at the sound of his name.

"Alistair? Alistair, where are you? Alistair Lecky!" Miss Hopper turned in circles, looking.

"He was here a minute ago, Miss." Stevie's hand shot up urgently with this bit of information. "He was right there where that white blob is on the floor!" Stevie almost toppled off the stage in his anxiety to show Miss Hopper the important blob.

She looked. "Yes, yes, I see the blob. But that isn't Alistair."

"Oh, Miss! Miss! Maybe it is, Miss," bawled Tessie Hogg. "He was there. I saw him too. He's vanished. That little white blob must be him.

Ooo-er, he's turned into crystals! He could have. I saw this film about –"

"Come now, Tessie. Let's be sensible. I think you see too many films." Miss Hopper couldn't help smiling.

Stevie was now alarmed at the loss of his friend. "He's got to be somewhere," he shouted, flying down from the stage. He ran the length of the hall and looked into the P.E. boxes. No Aly.

Other children scattered and looked outside the swing doors, behind the piano, in the wings, behind the folds of the stage curtains and in the adjoining kitchen. But no one could find Aly.

"We'll give him a few moments longer. Perhaps he's slipped out to the toilet without wanting to disturb us," Miss Hopper said, although the

children were not allowed to go without asking permission.

Aly stood so still inside the screen
he thought he was going to suffocate.
Maybe it would be better to suffocate
than be found as he was. They were
bound to find him sooner or later

and he didn't know what he would say. For a second he thought maybe he could turn it into a joke, like stepping out casually and saying, "Hello folks, just stepped in here for a few minutes. Anything wrong with that?"

But he realised the "wrong" part was not coming out when his teacher called him. He was wondering what the punishment would be when, at that same moment, Miss Hopper found a question-mark rising in her mind.

She was wondering whose feet were in the black shiny shoes peeping out under the medical screen. She

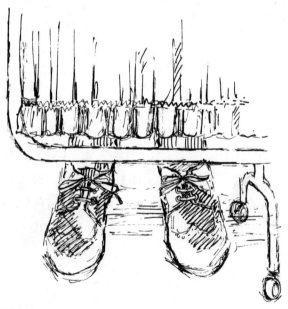

walked over. Carefully, with both
hands she drew the screen apart, as
though she was opening a pea-pod.

Aly didn't hear her coming. He couldn't see through the screen, but all at once light came pouring in. Miss Hopper's round face was there unsmiling, yet sympathetic as always.

"Alistair, what a strange place to be," she whispered, as though she was trying not to give him away. "Come along now. I think you should go and lie down, don't you?"

By this time, the whole of Class 2 was pushing about, trying to look into the screen, round the sides, and underneath, all except Reggie Barker who was still sitting in a puffed-out sulk.

It was Stevie who added more excitement to the discovery. "Miss Hopper? Why can't he be Swig – Aly? He's got glasses. He got them on

66

Saturday you know, so he could lose them and squint. I bet Aly could squint." Stevie was doing it very well himself as he gave an impersonation of Aly, before Saturday.

"Course he can," Tessie Hogg joined in. "He's been doing it for ages, I've seen him. You can Aly. You know you can." She sounded almost accusing as she lunged forward and pressed one finger into Aly's pullover.

Then twenty-eight children nodded in agreement and began to say, "We want Aly! We want Aly! We want Aly!" They went on and on until Miss Hopper held up her hand for silence.

"I'm absolutely sure Alistair could do it, splendidly. We all know he can act. But unfortunately he's not well.

67

I think he should be in bed." She put an arm round Aly's shoulder and drew him out from the screen. "I'm so sorry. I'll give your mother a ring at play-time."

But Aly's eyes had already lit up behind his spectacles. "I'm not," he said, brightly. "I'm not ill. I *was* this morning, but that was because – because – "

"Yes? Because of what, Alistair?" Miss Hopper prompted.

"Well – you see, the 'because' is better now. I'm fine. And I can squint, look." He took off his spectacles and squinted up at his teacher.

"Gr-r-r-reat," yelled Tessie Hogg. "He's a real squinter. I told you. Come on, Aly! Come on!" She tugged at Aly's pullover and ushered

him in front of her up the steps to the stage. Aly stumbled along trying to push his specs back on.

As Miss Hopper handed him the script she said, "Take your specs off when you can, Alistair. Remember now, you're *Swig-The-Squinter*."

"Yes, Miss Hopper," Aly smiled. And he was.

He was so good, Miss Hopper couldn't stop laughing right up to the end. His spiky hair was exactly right for the shocked look each time his spells went wrong. And he staggered about the poorly-lit stage when he took his specs off.

In the final scene, the Christmas-Cracker-Creeper was supposed to have grown all over his house, inside and out because the magician couldn't find the right spell to stop it. The swigs he took from his bottles and the magic words he tried to remember only increased its growth and produced explosions instead of bangs as the crackers popped apart. Six children with drums and cymbals from the percussion band made the explosions.

Tears of laughter were running

down Miss Hopper's cheeks as Aly
came to the final lines.

"And a Merry – " *Boom! Boom!
Boom!* "Christmas – " *Boom!* "to all
of you – " *Boom! Boom! Boom!* "And
a Happy – " *Boom!* "New Year!"
Boom! Boom! Boom!

Swig-The-Squinter finished by col-
lapsing on the floor with the
Christmas-Cracker-Creeper heaped
on top of him.

Miss Hopper clapped and said, "That was wonderful! I'm so glad you feel better Alistair. You see, I had you down for the part to begin with, until your mother spoke to me this morning."

Aly scrambled to his feet and jumped down from the stage. "My mother? She spoke to you? You mean it wasn't my specs and my hair and – you don't think I'm a freak?" The words came tumbling out, fast.

"A freak?" Miss Hopper repeated. "What *do* you mean, Alistair? How could you look like a freak? No, no, no, your mother said you had been feeling sick this morning, so I didn't think it was fair to expect you to act. In fact you were behaving rather oddly. I began to think you should go home, but you're better now. Or, perhaps your acting is better when you feel ill?'' she said, and half shut her eyes in a knowing way.

"I'm better, yes. But aren't my specs and my hair and my – "

"Alistair! You're just fine. Your spectacles suit you, I assure you. You remind me of someone on television. I know, it's that boy who played Brains in – in, oh, what was it called? I can't remember."

Tessie Hogg elbowed her way close and held on to Miss Hopper's arm. She pumped it up and down saying, "I know, I remember, Miss. It was called *Here Come The Double Deckers*. I know because my brother looks like Doughnut, the fat boy."

"That's it, Tessie," Miss Hopper beamed. "*Here Come The Double Deckers*. As I've said before, what

75

would I do without you?"

"You'd manage, Miss," Tessie said, generously. "My Mum couldn't though. She says I'm her Memory Bank."

Aly stood deep in thoughts that were filling up his mind. The Double Deckers – Brains and Doughnut. The names were familiar, but he couldn't picture the series. He was trying to sort it out in his mind when he heard Miss Hopper's voice. She was saying, "It's snowing heavily everyone and it's settling. We'll have wet play here in the hall. I'll just get my tea."

Chapter 6
Specs Forever O.K.?

AT THREE-FORTY, STEVIE and Aly left
school together. The snow was about
four centimetres deep. Small drifts
had formed by the school wall and
were being demolished for ammu-
nition as the children stock-piled
their snowballs.

The first ones out had made a long
snaky trail across the yard to the
gate. Aly put his spectacles in his
school-bag and joined on the end of
the slide with Stevie. It ended in a
collision with everyone bunched

round the gate. Aly and Stevie laughed as they were pelted with snowballs from every side. They dodged out through the gate-way.

"It's funny how a day can start out being the worst ever, then turn out to be one of the best," Aly said.

"Do you mean today?"

"Yes, today. Don't tell anybody

Stevie, but I was sick this morning because of my specs. I was terrified to come to school. I had nothing in my stomach but I could have been sick all over everywhere, I felt so bad about my specs. And I thought Miss Hopper hated the sight of me when she looked at me this morning. And everybody laughing at me – well, it was rotten. But by the end of the day, I've had a Kit Kat from Mrs Pearce, a part in the play and even people wanting me to get a part."

Stevie thought seriously for a moment and said, "My Dad says that nothing's ever as bad as it seems. Only you've got to remember that before, not after. Look there's your mother."

Aly's mother was standing at the crossing by the traffic lights. She looked anxious as she rubbed her gloves together. Aly could hardly wait to tell her his news. She was only half-way over by the island when he shouted.

"I got a part in the play! I'm Swig-The-Squinter!"

His mother's anxious look smoothed away. She didn't hear what he said, but she knew it was good news. Then she was with them and taking them quickly back across the road before the green man disappeared.

"Hello boys! That's a new anorak, isn't it Stevie?" she asked, noticing straight away.

Stevie was about to answer but Aly was too impatient. "Did you hear me, Mum? I'm Swig-The-Squinter in the Christmas play. Reggie Barker had it, then I got it."

"And I'm Swig's assistant," Stevie joined in.

Aly's mother slithered to a halt in the snow. "Who in the world is Swig-The-Squinter?" she laughed. "If I've got the name right."

The snowflakes were getting larger and tickling their faces as Aly and Stevie together tried to explain the plot of the school play.

Then Stevie stopped abruptly and clapped a hand over his mouth. "Oh, we shouldn't have told you, Mrs Lecky. Now it won't be a surprise."

"Don't worry, I'm sure it will," Aly's mother smiled. "School concerts are always full of surprises."

They had arrived at Stevie's turning into Hector Court. He said, "See you in the morning, Swigy Al! 'Bye Mrs Lecky," and zig-zagged away in

82

a snowy groove between the railings.

"See you," Aly called.

Then his mother said, "Well, how is it?"

"How's what?"

"The stomach."

"Oh, the stomach. That's fine. I wasn't sick. I'm fine." Aly opened his eyes as wide as they would go and added, "So are the specs. Specky-Lecky, that's me!"

In reply, his mother scooped up a handful of snow and threw it at him. "*That's* for feeling sick this morning," she shouted, and scooped up some more. "And *that's* for feeling better! And this one's for getting a part in the school play!"

Aly ducked away from the first two snowballs, but the third one hit him on the leg. And they went on firing snow at each other until they reached home.

His mother was out of breath when they came to their block of flats. "R-R-Reggie B-Barker couldn't have been very pleased," she panted.

"No, but his hippo hide was cracked for once. It was Miss Hopper who did

it. Nobody else could," Aly said. He felt a bit sorry for Reggie, but only a bit.

"Oh dear me! I'm exhausted." Aly's mother put the key in the lock and flung the door open.

As Aly shook off his anorak and boots, he remembered something he had completely forgotten about for two days.

"Like a cup of tea to warm you up?" his mother asked.

"Yes please. But first, I've got a date with a Gnu." He hopped and jumped along the hall in his socks, humming the tune of the Gnu jingle.

He opened his bedroom window, pushing hard against the tightly packed snow. It was still there. His Gnu bar was buried in a tomb of glistening white snow. Prising it up from the wooden ledge, he rubbed the snow from the wrapper.

Slowly the blue lettering appeared, then the brown face of the gnu. He was about to turn it over and tear off the wrapper when he looked again at the gnu. The animal was grinning and there, across the end of its nose were – spectacles. The gnu was wearing spectacles and he had never noticed before. Or maybe, Aly thought, he just hadn't been able to see them properly before.

But, a gnu in specs! Somebody had actually sat down and thought that if you put a gnu on a sweet wrapper and gave it specs, people would like it and want to buy the sweet. The specs were an added attraction.

Aly let the idea sink in for a few seconds, then he thought of people he

knew with the same added attrac-
tions. There was no one else in his
class with specs but, as he went on
thinking, a row of faces slid by, like
the gifts in one of those give-away
television programmes. He saw,

Kenneth Kendall reading the news, Eric Morecombe pushing his specs up and cracking jokes, Arthur C. Clarke talking about great mysteries, James Burke racing through general knowledge. They moved along one by one.

Then Aly saw a den with tyre-swings, loads of junk and children singing. There was Doughnut, Scooper, Spring, Tiger and the boy Brains – with specs. The Double Deckers fitted into place at last. Next, Aly saw himself, as if he had stepped out of his skin. He was look-ing at his own face gliding by in specs and he didn't look funny at all.

He leaned close to the mirror over his chest of drawers and gazed at his reflection. The hair didn't look quite as bad as before, and it would grow.

And, if he looked carefully, he could see the pearly glint of two new teeth pushing through his pink gums.

Aly smiled, drew his Schoolboy's Diary from his pocket and wrote in the space for Monday, Specks Specs Forever O.K.? The question mark

Specks   Specs Forever O.K?
                    N. M. F

had a long tail on it as Aly's hand jerked at the sound of his mother's voice.

"Tea's ready! Come and get it while it's hot!"

"Co-o-o-oming!" Aly replied, pitching his voice as high as he could. Then he turned the tail of the question mark into an arrow and wrote,

N.M.F. That meant, *Not My Fault*.
Still in his socks and holding the Gnu
bar, he hopped along to the kitchen
singing,

"You can chew, chew, chew,
    On a Gnu, nu-nu,
    No matter where you are,
    No matter what you do,
    Chew a Gnu, chew a Gnu, chew a
    Gnu."

His mother was pouring milk into
the tea cups. By the time she looked
up, Aly had pushed his specs down to
the end of his nose. He gave his
mother a mischievous grin, as much
like the gnu on the Gnu as he could
manage.